BILLY AND THE MINI MONSTERS

MONSTERS GO BACK TO SCHOOL

ZANNA DAVIDSON • Illustrated by MELANIE WILLIAMSON

Meet Billy...

Billy was just an ordinary boy living an ordinary life, until **ONE NIGHT** he found five **MINI MONSTERS** in his sock drawer.

Gloop   Peep   Fang-Face   Captain Snott   Trumpet

Then he saved their lives, and they swore never to leave him.

We give you the Secret-Hairy-Snot-Tooth Oath of Devotion.

When he moved house, Billy found ANOTHER monster.

Hello. My name's Sparkle-Bogey.

One thing was certain – Billy's life would never be the same **AGAIN**...

Contents

Chapter 1
The Worry List … 5

Chapter 2
The Shopping Trip … 20

Chapter 3
Missing Monsters … 32

Chapter 4
First Day Back … 44

Chapter 5
The New Boy … 56

Chapter 6
Mini Monster School … 68

Chapter 1
The Worry List

"Humph!" thought Billy. It was nearly the end of the summer holidays. In just **two days** he would be BACK AT SCHOOL.

His mum was busy checking his **school clothes.** None of them seemed to fit.

...EVEN your shoes!

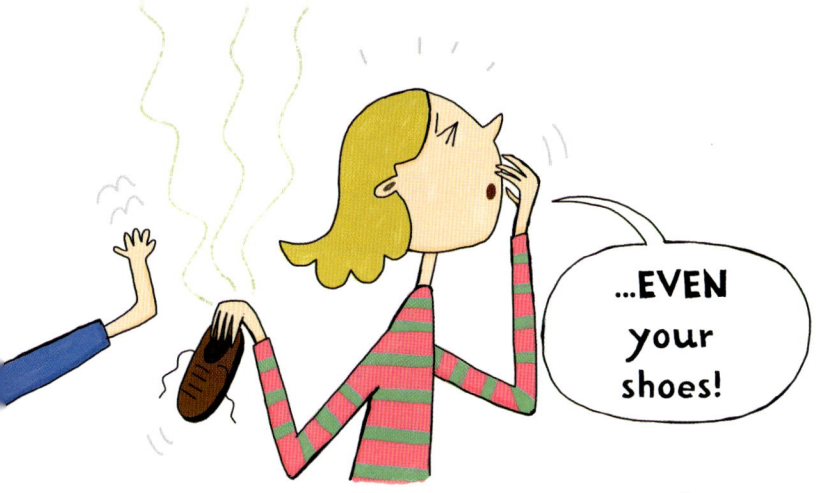

"And what are all these **holes** in your socks?"

"*My* socks don't have holes in them," said Billy's sister, Ruby.

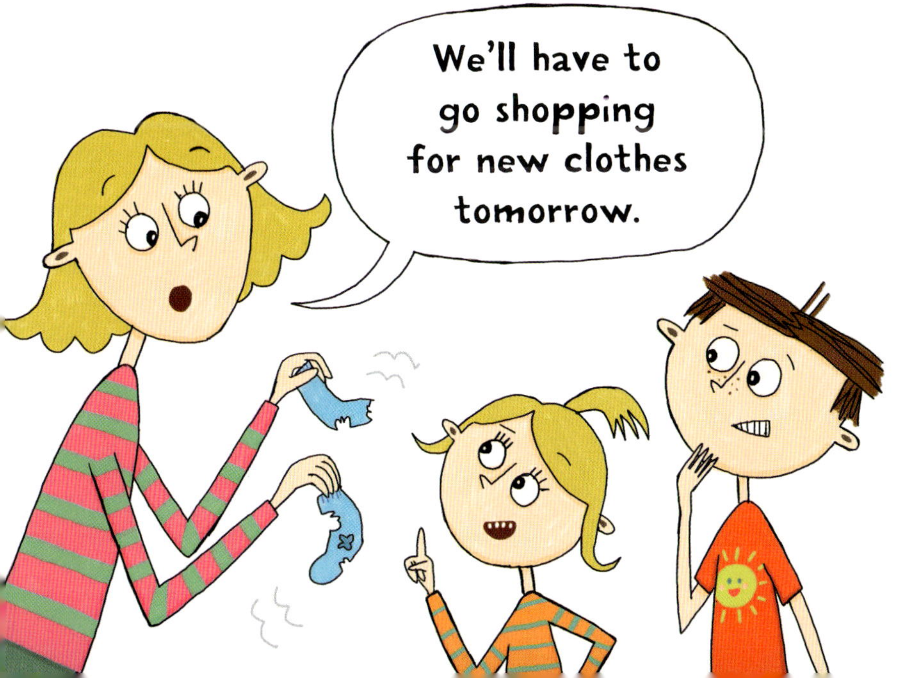
We'll have to go shopping for new clothes tomorrow.

"Um... I think I might have lost my pencil case, too," said Billy.

"I'll add it to the list," sighed his mum. Then she looked at his tie...

And your tie!

SHOPPING LIST for Billy

* NEW school trousers
* NEW school shirt
* NEW school jumper
* NEW school shoes
* NEW school tie
* NEW school pencil case

After Billy's mum and Ruby had left the room, the **Mini Monsters** came out from their sock drawer.

"Fang-Face, did you eat my socks and tie?" said Billy.

> I tried not to... but they're SO DELICIOUS.

"Ooh! Are you excited about going back to school, Billy?" asked Trumpet.

"A bit of me is excited," said Billy. "But **a lot** of me is worried. In fact, I wrote my worries down, but I don't think it helped..."

MY LIST OF WORRIES

1. I won't like my new school clothes. They will be STIFF and ITCHY.

2. I REALLY want a cool new pencil case, but what if I don't get the right one?

Dream pencil case

Pencil case I will probably get

3. What if my new form teacher is Ms. Grimes? Everyone says her eyes can SHOOT LASERS...

...and when she gets angry, her NOSTRILS get so enormous they're like BLACK HOLES that can SWALLOW YOU WHOLE.

4. Worst worry of all — what if Ash and I aren't in the same class? We always sit together. Will the teachers BREAK US UP????

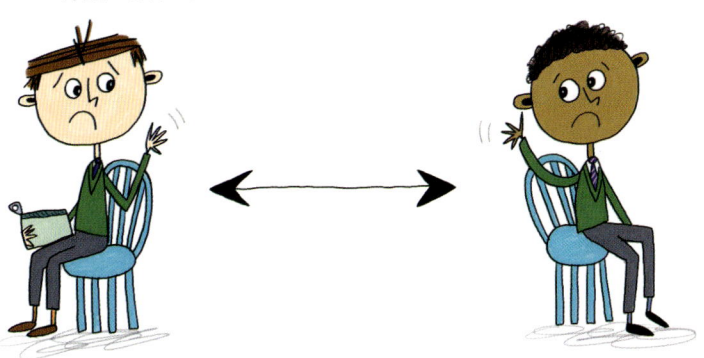

"I'm sure everything will be okay at school, Billy," said Gloop.

"It will be," said Sparkle-Bogey, "because you are **BRAVE** and **STRONG**."

"Er, thanks," said Billy.

Then Billy noticed that Peep was looking really sad.

"What's happened, Peep?" asked Billy.

"I want to be able to go to school," said Peep.

"Oh!" said Billy. "But last time you came, it was a **disaster**..."

The Mini Monsters **definitely** weren't coming to school with him. But Billy wanted to find another way to cheer up Peep.

"I know!" he said. "I'm going to make **A SCHOOL FOR MINI MONSTERS.**"

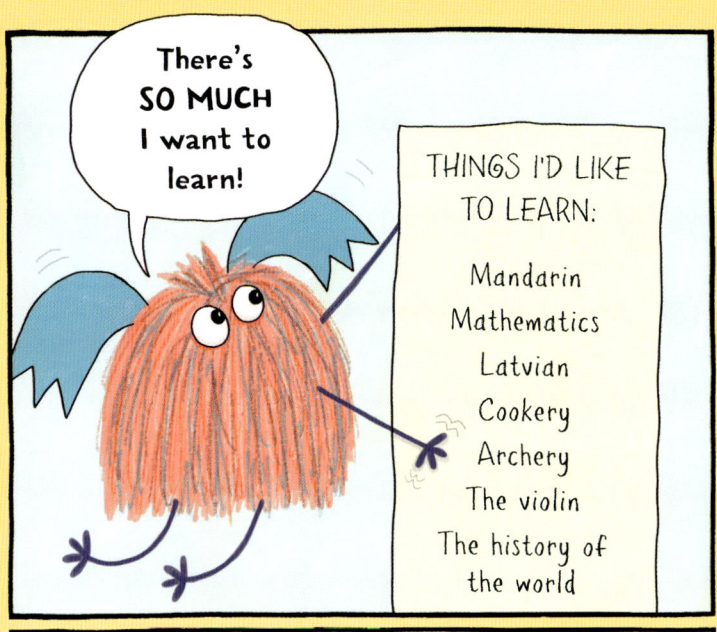

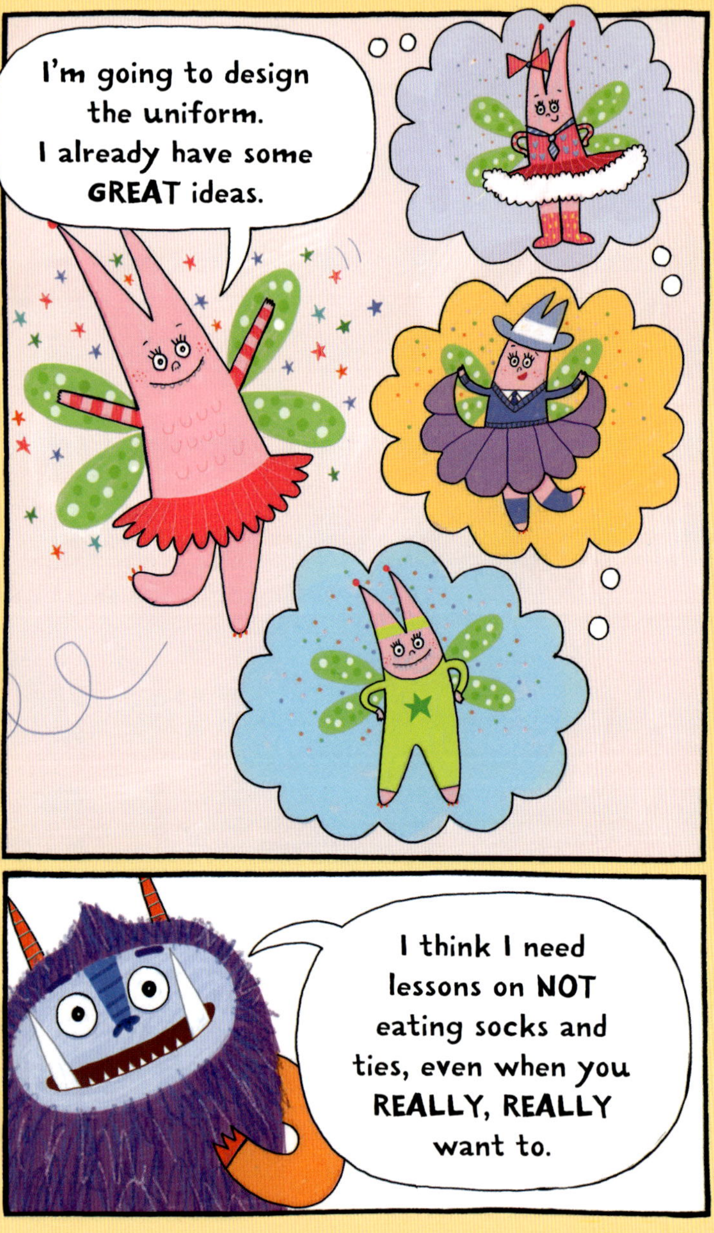

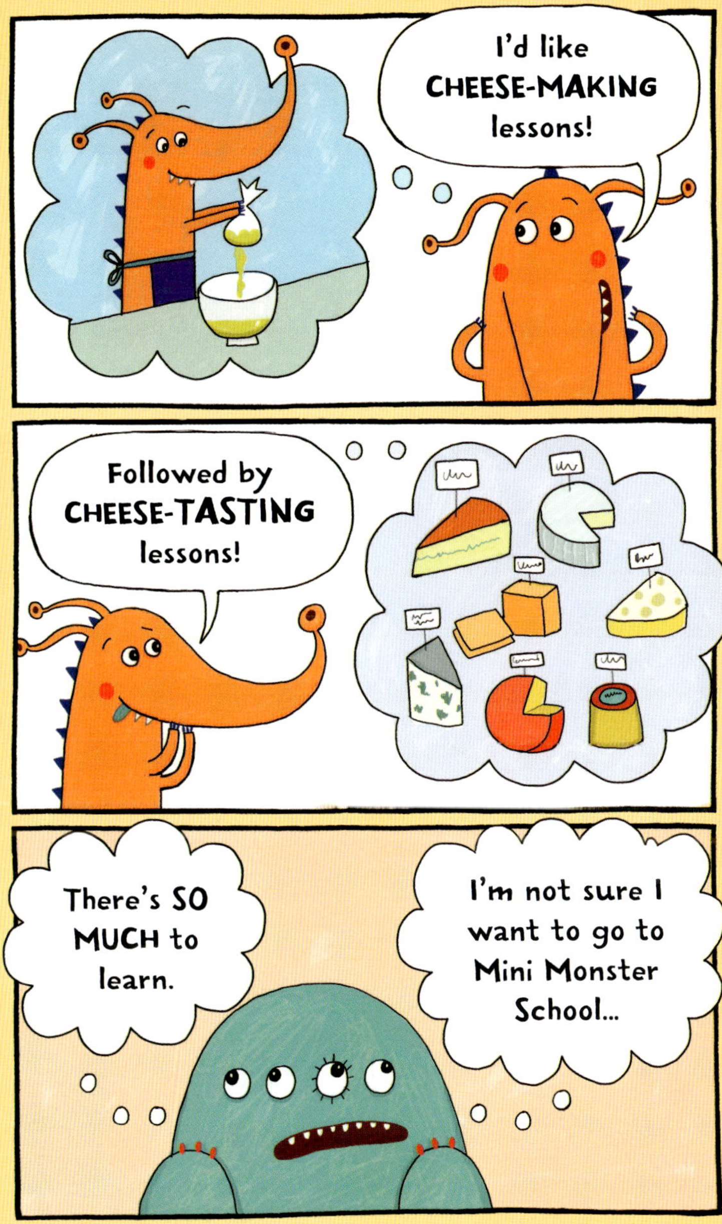

Chapter 2
The Shopping Trip

The next morning, Billy and his mum set out on their shopping trip. Billy invited the **Mini Monsters** to come too.

Into Billy's bag, everyone!

First stop was the uniform shop. Billy's mum bought him new shirts, new trousers, a new jumper and a new tie...

"They're perfect! It means you'll have **ROOM TO GROW**," said Billy's mum. "Everyone else's uniform will be just the same."

Billy spotted another boy in the shop, buying **exactly** the same uniform – though the other boy's uniform didn't seem to be **ten sizes** too big for him.

"Hi," said Billy. "Maybe we'll be in the same class! Are you feeling okay about starting a new school?"

"Yeah," said Ryan. "I'm feeling **really** excited."

After the clothes shopping, Billy and his mum went to the stationery shop. There were lots of **amazing** pencil cases.

A baby alien pencil case with a zip for a mouth...

...a football pencil case...

...a superhero pencil case with loads of different compartments...

...a racing car pencil case with ACTUAL wheels...

And, best of all, the pencil case Billy had ALWAYS wanted...

Billy looked over and saw that Ryan was in the stationery shop too, eyeing up the **SAME** pencil case.

"I'm sorry, Billy," said his mum, "but all these pencil cases are much too expensive."

And you'll only lose it anyway. This is the one we should get.

Okay, Mum.

"This shopping trip has been a **disaster**," Billy realized.

He now had **two new worries** to add to his list.

MY LIST OF WORRIES

5. Will everyone laugh at me because I've got a LOSER pencil case?

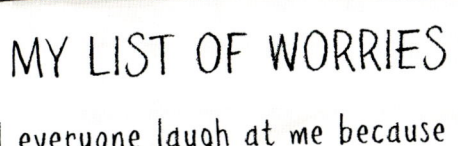

6. Will they laugh at me EVEN MORE because my clothes would fit a small giant?

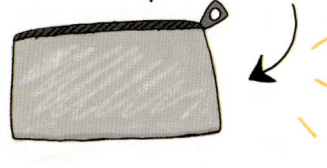

Then, as he put his new pencil case in his rucksack, Billy realized that the **Mini Monsters** were MISSING!

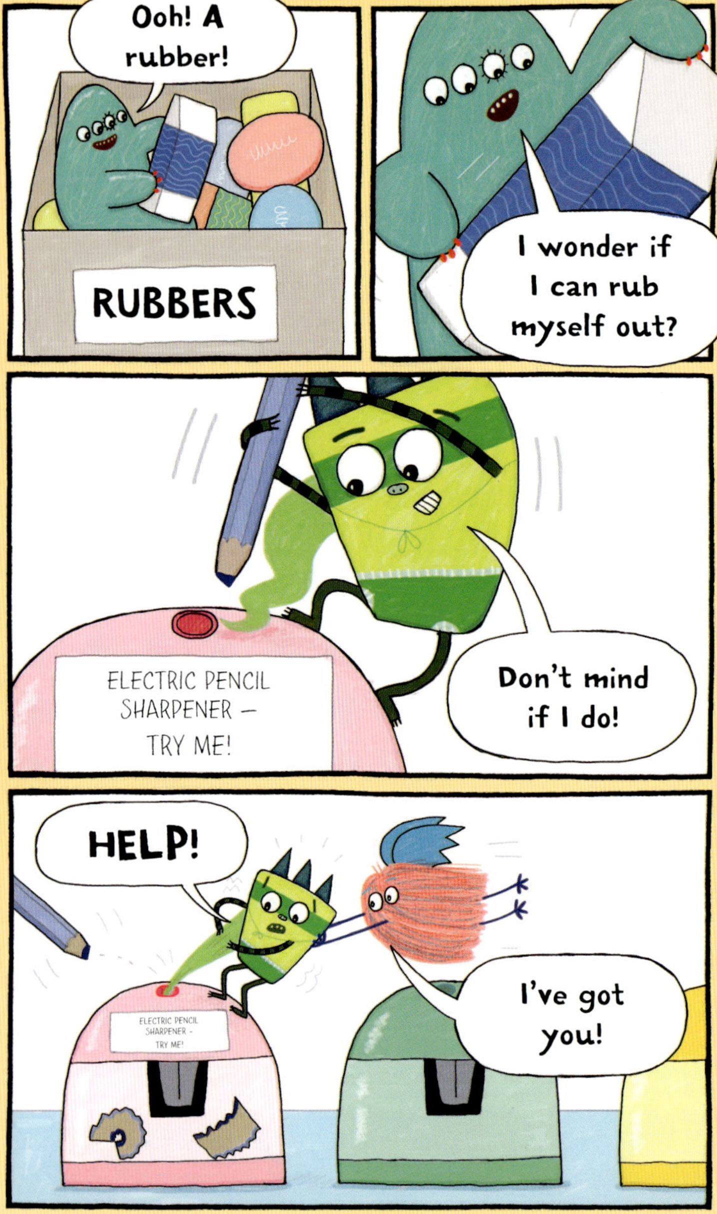

Chapter 3
Missing Monsters

Billy couldn't see his Mini Monsters **ANYWHERE**.

Now Billy had an EXTRA BIG WORRY to add to his worry list.

As soon as they got back, Billy raced over to Ash's house to tell him what had happened.

Ash was in the garden with Moss, the new **Mini Monster**, who had arrived at Easter.

"The **Mini Monsters** will find their way back to you," said Moss, after Billy had told them everything.

"But the shop is **REALLY** far away!" said Billy.

> Don't forget – Mini Monsters are VERY clever.

Billy had a think about all the ways his **Mini Monsters** had found their way back to him in the past.

Gloop escaped from a swimming pool DRAIN...

"How are you feeling about going back to school?" Billy asked Ash, as they began playing football.

"I'm **SO EXCITED!** I'm going to take Moss with me," said Ash.

"It'll be my first time **EVER** going to school with a Mini Monster!" Ash went on.

When Billy got home, he was starting to feel **cross**.

To stop himself from thinking about it, Billy decided to get to work on his **Mini Monster School**.

He made classrooms out of shoe boxes...

...tiny tables and chairs out of cardboard...

...and drew some posters for the walls.

But it still took Billy a long time to get to sleep that night. He was wondering if he'd **ever** see his Mini Monsters again.

Where could they be?

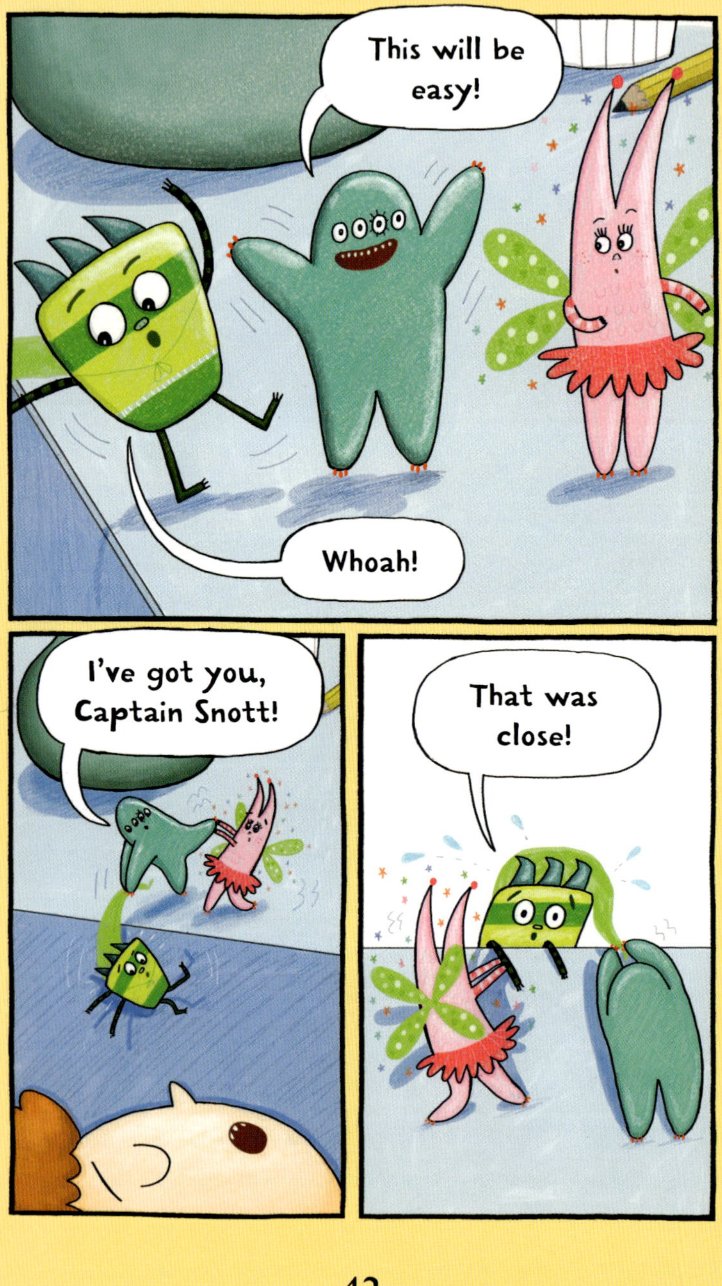

Chapter 4
First Day Back

Billy knew IMMEDIATELY that his first day back was going to be a **DISASTER**.

No one else's uniform was as big as his.

No one else had a BORING pencil case.

He wasn't in the same class as Ash. Ash had really-nice-Mr.-Wright, who told jokes that were actually funny.

Instead, he was in a class with Ms. Grimes and her **ENORMOUS NOSTRILS.**

ARGH!

At least, Billy told himself, things couldn't get any worse. But it turned out he was **WRONG**...

Ryan, the new boy, started making jokes about Billy's uniform...

Is anyone in there?

...and his pencil case.

First prize for the MOST BORING pencil case!

Everyone was laughing. Billy was worried that he might cry. He tried thinking about what Sparkle-Bogey had said to him.

"I AM brave and strong," thought Billy. "I'm not going to let Ryan upset me."

Then, out of the corner of his eye, Billy saw something **STRANGE**...

Ryan's pencil case was **moving** across his desk. While Ryan was busy laughing, it reached the edge...

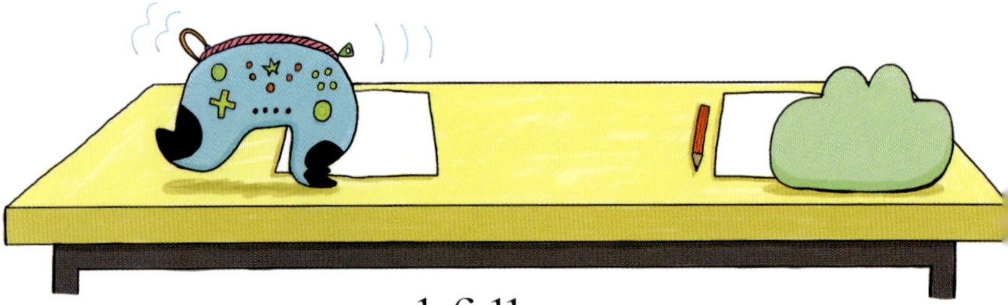

...and fell...

Wheeee

...onto the floor.

Now it was moving **across the floor** towards Billy's bag. Billy's eyes were on stalks!

Finally, the pencil case CATAPULTED itself into his BAG.

Is it a magic pencil case?

A remote control pencil case?

Or... MY MINI MONSTERS!

Ryan stopped laughing and looked at his desk. "Who's taken my pencil case?" he asked, **very loudly**.

Billy **FROZE**.
What was he going to do?

Billy looked up. Ms. Grimes' eyes lasered into him...

Next, she flared her **GINORMOUS** nostrils. Was he going to be sucked into them?

ARGH!

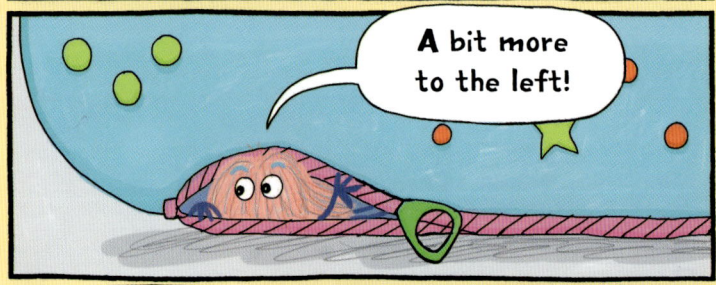

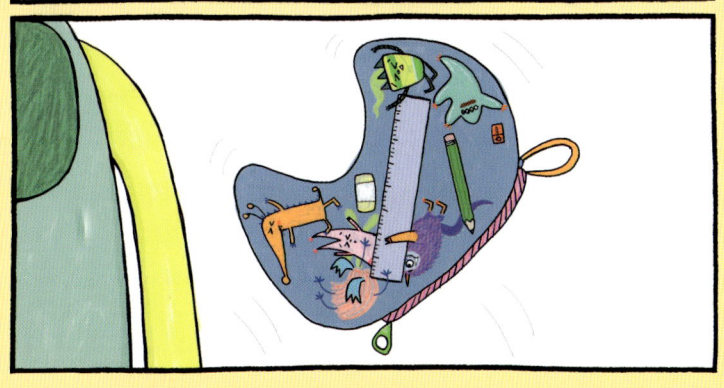

Chapter 5
The New Boy

"Open up your bag, please, Billy," said Ms. Grimes.

"Yikes!" thought Billy. He was pretty sure the pencil case *and* the Mini Monsters were **inside** his bag.

He thought through his choices.

a) Open my bag — but then Ms. Grimes will think I've STOLEN the pencil case AND she might DISCOVER the MINI MONSTERS and suck THEM up her nostrils.

b) REFUSE to open up my bag and risk being lasered by Ms. Grimes' laser eyes.

OR

c) Come up with a CUNNING DISTRACTION.

"If only I could think of a cunning distraction!"

Suddenly there was a loud SHOUT and the classroom door BANGED open. It was Mr. Wright, looking a bit green.

"Ms. Grimes," said Mr. Wright. "There's a tiny **MONSTER** in my classroom. You have to come and see this."

"Oh no!" thought Billy, as everyone raced to the door. "I bet that's Moss!"

Soon, only Ryan and Billy were left in the classroom.

As Ryan stared at him, Billy could see the Mini Monsters spilling out of the pencil case...

Come on, everyone! Next, we need to get the pencil case back to Ryan.

Help me drag it across the floor.

I am helping! I just have weak arms.

"You did take my pencil case, didn't you?" said Ryan.

"I really didn't!" said Billy. "Look, isn't that it, over there?"

Then Billy remembered something he'd learned about bullies at his last school. They're usually **scared** of something.

Ryan handed Billy his pencil case. "I'd like you to have this. We can swap."

Billy grinned. "Thanks," he said. "But I've just realized something. I don't *need* your pencil case."

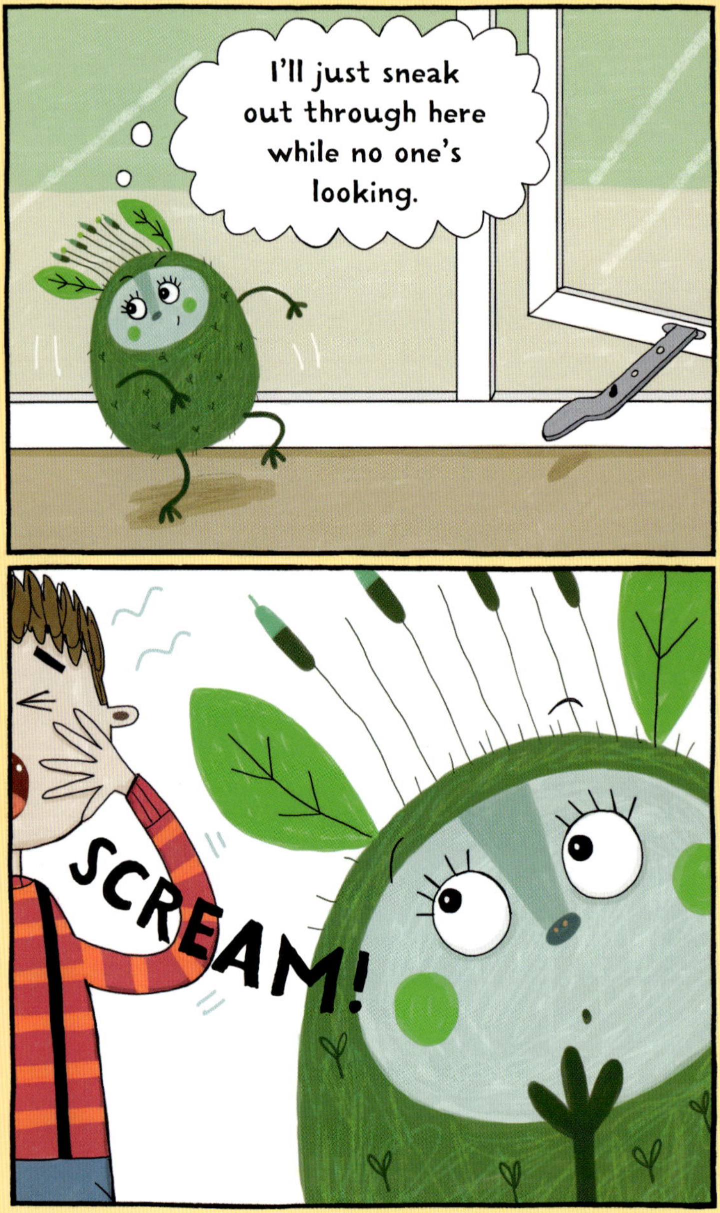

Chapter 6
Mini Monster School

By the time Billy and Ryan arrived in the classroom, Mr. Wright was scratching his head.

"Everyone outside," ordered Ms. Grimes. "Mr. Wright, you and I should have a *chat*..."

In the playground, Billy found Ash, looking in the flowerbed under the window.

Ash carefully put Moss in his pocket, before anyone else could spot her.

"I found my Mini Monsters, too," Billy told Ash.

"That's great," said Ash. Then he gave a wobbly smile.

"I'm having a bit of a tricky day," he said.

"I thought we'd be in the same class, like last year," Ash went on.

"At least we've got breaktime together," Billy pointed out.

And we can hang out together after school!

"That's true," said Ash. "We'll still be **BEST FRIENDS**... won't we?"

"Definitely!" said Billy.

At the end of the day, Billy's dad was there to collect him.

After tea, Ash came over with Moss, and Billy showed the **Mini Monsters** their new school.

"What's our first lesson going to be?" asked Peep.

"It's going to be about POSITIVITY!" said Billy. "Because that's the best lesson I learned today. Sparkle-Bogey, do you want to read from your book?"

Then came a shout from downstairs.

Billy!

cried his mum.

The Mini Monsters all hid as the door opened.

"What have you done to your old uniform? I was going to take these to the second-hand shop!"

What have you got to say for yourself?

As she turned to go, Gloop whispered in Billy's ear.

"Oh, I know!" said Billy. "*My mistakes help me learn and grow!*"

"Really, Billy!" sighed his mum, as she went out of the door.

I AM good at Mini Monster School. Hooray!

All about the MINI MONSTERS

CAPTAIN SNOTT →

LIKES EATING: bogeys.

SPECIAL SKILL: can glow in the dark.

SCARE FACTOR: 5/10

← GLOOP

LIKES EATING: cake.

SPECIAL SKILL: very stre-e-e-tchy. Gloop can also swallow his own eyeballs and make them reappear on any part of his body.

SCARE FACTOR: 4/10

FANG-FACE →

LIKES EATING: socks, school ties, paper, or anything that comes his way.

SPECIAL SKILL: has massive fangs.

SCARE FACTOR: 9/10

TRUMPET

LIKES EATING: vegan cheese.

SPECIAL SKILL: amazingly powerful cheese-powered parps.

SCARE FACTOR: 7/10

(taking into account his parps)

PEEP

LIKES EATING: very small flies.

SPECIAL SKILL: can fly (but not very far, or very well).

SCARE FACTOR: 0/10 (unless you're afraid of small hairy things)

SPARKLE-BOGEY

LIKES EATING: eco-glitter and bogeys.

SPECIAL SKILL: can shoot out clouds of glitter.

SCARE FACTOR: 5/10 (if you're scared of sparkly glitter)

← MOSS

LIKES EATING: Easter eggs.

SPECIAL SKILL: can survive outside in all weathers. Excellent at looking like a clump of moss.

SCARE FACTOR: 4/10
(if she takes you by surprise)

Series editors: Lesley Sims and Becky Walker
Series designer: Brenda Cole
Cover design by Hannah Cobley

First published in 2025. Copyright © 2025 Usborne Publishing Limited. The name Usborne and the Balloon logo are registered trade marks of Usborne Publishing Limited. All rights reserved.

No part of this publication may be reproduced or used in any manner for the purpose of training artificial intelligence technologies or systems (including for text or data mining), stored in retrieval systems or transmitted in any form or by any means without prior permission of the publisher. UKE.